"Ready! Set! Go!" sho[shouted] Sagwa and her brother, D[Dongwa,] playing tag with their little sister, Sheegwa.

"I won! I won!" cried Sagwa.

"You were just lucky," replied Dongwa. "Right, Sheegwa?" Dongwa looked around for his little sister.

Sheegwa was playing a new game. "Hello, butterfly!" she said.

The butterfly darted around her head.

Sheegwa chased it. She tried to jump as high as the butterfly flew.

PRINCESS SHEEGWA

By George Daugherty
Illustrations by Gretchen Schields

Based on the screenplay "Princess Sheegwa," written by
Anne-Marie Perrota and Tean Schultz

Illustrations based on storyboards by Elie Klimos

SCHOLASTIC INC.
New York   Toronto   London   Auckland   Sydney
Mexico City   New Delhi   Hong Kong   Buenos Aires

ISBN 0-439-42880-7

12 11 10 9 8 7 6 5 4   3 4 5 6/0

Printed in the U.S.A.
First Scholastic printing, October 2002

PLOP! Sheegwa didn't see Tai-Tai and the Foolish Magistrate. They were in the pagoda with an important guest, a diplomat from Beijing.

"What is this animal doing here?"
cried Tai-Tai.

The Foolish Magistrate picked up
Sheegwa. He tickled her under the chin.
"Why, my dear, it's only our
sweet little kitten," he said.

"Well, she needs to be a careful kitten," grumbled Tai-Tai. But then Tai-Tai started to laugh.

Sheegwa was so cute. Nobody could stay mad at her.

The man from Beijing looked at Sheegwa. He pointed to a mark on her cheek.

It was shaped like a star.

"This is very interesting!" he said. He took a closer look.

"I never noticed that mark before," Tai-Tai said.

Suddenly, the man from Beijing gasped. "You should be thrilled!" he exclaimed.

"Do you know what this mark is? It's the star of the princess!" he said with great importance.

"Yes," said Tai-Tai, getting excited. "I do remember an ancient Chinese prophecy. 'Anyone born with this star is a princess'!"

"But she's a KITTEN!" shouted the Foolish Magistrate.

"It does not matter!" said the man. "Your kitten was born with the star."

"My goodness," exclaimed Tai-Tai. "Our little Sheegwa is a PRINCESS kitten!"

The next day, Tai-Tai and the Foolish Magistrate gave a great party for Princess Sheegwa. Sheegwa sat on a very fancy pillow. She wore very fancy robes. Everybody had to bow to her. Even Sagwa and Dongwa!

Tai-Tai served Sheegwa her food.
Everybody in the palace showered
Sheegwa with wonderful gifts and
delicious treats.
Everybody seemed happy for Sheegwa.
Well, everybody except Sagwa.

"I can't believe Sheegwa is going to get all the good stuff. It's not fair." Sagwa sighed.

"Sagwa! Don't be jealous!" said Mama Miao. "You should be happy for your sister."

But Sagwa couldn't help feeling jealous. Sheegwa was getting everything, and Sagwa could only watch. Finally, she snuck outside.

Out in the garden, Fu-Fu flew down to greet Sagwa. "It is so exciting that Sheegwa is a princess!" exclaimed Fu-Fu.

"It should have been me!" blurted out Sagwa. "I should have been the princess! I'm older, I'm faster, I'm smarter!"

"But Sheegwa was born with the star," said Fu-Fu. "You should be happy for her."

"Why should I?" exclaimed Sagwa.

"Because she's your sister," said Fu-Fu quietly. "And she's always been happy whenever something good happened to *you*."

Sagwa thought for a
moment. "You're right,
Fu-Fu," she said. "I should
be happy for her." And she
scampered back into the palace.

But in the palace,
Sheegwa was bored.
She had eaten too
much. And she
was tired of just sitting
while everybody bowed
to her.

As soon as Sheegwa saw Sagwa, she jumped off the pillow and ran over to her big sister.

"Come on, Sagwa. Let's go outside and play! I don't want to be a princess anymore!"

Everybody in the room gasped. The guest from Beijing rushed over. "But, Your Royal Highness, you have no choice. You are the princess! You were born with the star!"

"Exactly," said Tai-Tai. "So you must ACT like a princess! You can't play with Sagwa anymore."

"But it's NO FUN being a princess!" Sheegwa started to cry. "I want to play with Sagwa! I want to play with Dongwa!"

Sagwa couldn't understand.
Sheegwa had everything. But her little
sister just cried harder and harder. Tears
rolled down her cheek. Right over the star
of the princess!

And then, to everybody's amazement, the star became lighter and lighter. The more Sheegwa cried, the lighter it got, until it faded away completely.

"It was only mud on her cheek!" exclaimed the man from Beijing. "She isn't a princess at all!"

"Not a princess? Not even a little tiny bit?" whispered Tai-Tai, brokenhearted.

Before Tai-Tai
could say another word,
Sheegwa darted into the garden.
Sagwa ran after her.

"Help me get out of these robes," said Sheegwa.

"But they're so beautiful!" said Sagwa.

"They're hot and itchy!" answered Sheegwa. "I don't like them!"

"But what about all the presents? And all the food?" said Sagwa. "I was so jealous of you!"

"You were jealous of me?" said Sheegwa.

"Yes, I was," said Sagwa quietly. "I'm sorry I wasn't happy for you. I'm sorry you're not a princess anymore."

Sheegwa thought for a second.
"Well, I'm not sorry! Being a princess was
no fun! For me, the best thing is being
your little sister. Come on, let's play
tag!"

"You're It!" Sheegwa said. "Bet you can't catch me!" Sagwa happily chased after her.

GLOSSARY

Sagwa:
melon head.

Sheegwa:
watermelon.

Beijing:
the capital city of China;
it used to be called Peking.

Diplomat:
someone, like an ambassador, whose
job is to represent the government.

Magistrate:
a person whose job
it is to make and
enforce the law.

Prophecy:
a prediction, or guess, about the future.